ELEPHANT HAS A BROTHER

Written by Sue Graves

Illustrated by Trevor Dunton

W
FRANKLIN WATTS
LONDON • SYDNEY

On Saturday, Elephant's baby brother arrived. The grown-ups were very excited. Mum said he was **cuddly**. Grandma said he was **cute**. Dad said he was **handsome**.

But Elephant didn't think it would be fun at all.
He didn't want to share his toys or his games.
Worse still, **he didn't want to share**
Mum, Dad or Grandma!

Elephant got crosser and crosser. His little brother took up a lot of **everyone's time**. When he asked Mum to play football, she said she was **too busy**. She said she had to bath the baby. She said she would **play later**.

When he asked Dad to help him build
a toy boat, Dad said he was **too busy**.
He said he had to get the baby to sleep.
He said he would **help him later**.

When Elephant wanted to play a board game with Grandma, she said she was too busy. She said she had to knit a blanket for the baby. She said a blanket would keep the baby warm. She said she would **play later**.

Elephant said it **wasn't fair**. He said he wanted to do things **now**, not later. He said he wished **he didn't have a brother** at all!

Elephant went to find Monkey. He told him all his worries. He said he thought everyone liked the baby more than they liked him! He said no one had **time for him** anymore. Monkey said he **felt jealous** when his little sister arrived. He said everyone made such a fuss of her. He said at first he didn't want a sister.

Elephant was surprised. Monkey's sister **was nice**, and she and Monkey had lots of fun together.

Then Monkey told Elephant that,
one day, his little sister started to cry.
Monkey **was worried**.

18

He **remembered** that Mum rocked the cradle when she cried. He rocked the cradle. His little sister stopped crying! Monkey **felt pleased**.

Then Monkey **smiled** at her, and his little sister **smiled back**! Monkey was even more pleased. Then Monkey made lots of funny faces. His little sister laughed and laughed. It made Monkey laugh, too.

Mum said Monkey was **very kind** to look after his little sister so nicely. Monkey **felt proud**. After that, he helped look after his sister all the time. He felt grown-up helping his mum and dad. He said it was nice being a big brother.

Elephant had a think. He said he **wanted to feel grown-up**, too. He said he could **help** with the baby. Monkey said that was **a very good idea**.

Elephant helped Mum bath the baby.

Elephant helped
Dad get the baby
to sleep.

Elephant helped Grandma with her knitting.

26

Elephant even **shared his teddy** with his brother! His brother smiled a big smile at Elephant. Elephant said he was **glad** he had a baby brother. He said brothers were **good fun**!

A note about sharing this book

The *Experiences Matter* series has been developed to provide a starting point for further discussion on how children might deal with new experiences. It provides opportunities to explore ways of developing coping strategies as they face new challenges. The series is set in the jungle with animal characters reflecting typical behaviour traits and attitudes often seen in young children.

Elephant Has a Brother
This story looks at some of the most common worries and insecurities children face when a new sibling is introduced into the family. It also suggests ways in which they can overcome their concerns and help them to accept the new arrival more readily.

How to use the book
The book is designed for adults to share with either an individual child, or a group of children, and as a starting point for discussion.

The book also provides visual support and repeated words and phrases to build reading confidence.

Before reading the story
Choose a time to read when you and the children are relaxed and have time to share the story.

Spend time looking at the illustrations and talk about what the book might be about before reading it together.

Encourage children to employ a phonics first approach to tackling new words by sounding the words out.

After reading, talk about the book with the children:

- Talk about the story with the children. What is the story about?
  Why do the children think Elephant didn't like his baby brother at first?
  Who did Elephant talk to about his worries? How did Monkey help Elephant?

- Ask the children if they have younger brothers and sisters.
  Can they recall how they felt when the new baby came into the home?
  Did they feel jealous at all? Why?

- How many felt that the new baby took up too much time?
  Did they feel annoyed sometimes that Mum, Dad or their carer
  couldn't play with them as often as they did before the baby arrived?

- How many enjoyed helping with the new baby? What sort of things did
  they help with? How did it make them feel? Invite the children to share
  their experiences with the others.

- Ask the children to draw pictures of themselves helping their carers with a
  new baby. If they don't have younger brothers and sisters, ask them to
  imagine how they would help at home if they did. Ask them to write two or
  three sentences about how they would help. Be mindful that some children
  may really want a younger sibling but are not be able to have one.
  If appropriate, the conversation could widen into how families are not made
  up of a certain number of people and what is important in families is love
  and time spent together.
  You could look at examples
  from the story where the family
  is showing this.

- At the end of the session, invite
  some of the children to show
  their pictures to the others
  and to read out their sentences.

29

For Isabelle, William A, William G, George, Max, Emily, Leo, Caspar, Felix, Tabitha, Phoebe , Harry and Libby –S.G.

Franklin Watts
First published in 2021 by
The Watts Publishing Group

Text © Franklin Watts 2021
Illustrations © Trevor Dunton 2021

The right of Trevor Dunton to be identified as the illustrator
of this Work has been asserted in accordance with the
Copyright, Designs and Patents Act, 1988.

Editor: Jackie Hamley
Designer: Cathryn Gilbert

A CIP catalogue record for this book is available
from the British Library.

ISBN 978 1 4451 7326 9 (hardback)
ISBN 978 1 4451 7327 6 (paperback)

Printed in China

Franklin Watts is a division of
Hachette Children's Books,
an Hachette UK company.
www.hachette.co.uk

MIX
Paper from
responsible sources
FSC® C104740

FSC
www.fsc.org